BATTLE IN THE OVERWORLD

BATTLE IN THE OVERWORLD

MINECRAFTERS ACADEMY

BOOK THREE

Winter Morgan

Sky Pony Press
New York

Copyright © 2016 by Hollan Publishing, Inc.

Minecraft® is a registered trademark of Notch Development AB.

The Minecraft game is copyright © Mojang AB.

Sky Pony Press books may be purchased in bulk at special discounts for sales promotion, corporate gifts, fund-raising, or educational purposes. Special editions can also be created to specifications. For details, contact the Special Sales Department, Sky Pony Press, 307 West 36th Street, 11th Floor, New York, NY 10018 or info@skyhorsepublishing.com.

Sky Pony® is a registered trademark of Skyhorse Publishing, Inc.®, a Delaware corporation.

Minecraft® is a registered trademark of Notch Development AB.
The Minecraft game is copyright © Mojang AB.

Visit our website at www.skyponypress.com.

10 9 8 7 6 5 4 3 2 1

Library of Congress Cataloging-in-Publication Data is available on file.

Cover design by Brian Peterson
Cover photo by Megan Miller

Print ISBN: 978-1-5107-0596-8
Ebook ISBN: 978-1-5107-0606-4

Printed in Canada

TABLE OF CONTENTS

BATTLE IN THE OVERWORLD

Chapter 1
THE SPEECH

"Can I read it to you?" asked Lucy.

"Again?" Phoebe whined.

"Lucy, we've heard this speech about twenty million times." Jane was exaggerating, but they had heard Lucy recite her graduation speech a lot.

"I know, but I'm really nervous. Also I changed some of it and want to see what you think," Lucy explained. She had spent the last week reworking and revising the speech. Lucy was nervous about standing on stage and reading what she'd written in front of the large crowd. She wasn't a fan of speaking in public. The only time she had to be on stage was when she helped her friend Adam at the school talent show, acting as his assistant. Lucy remembered it that it hadn't been as bad as she had thought it would be, but she still preferred to work behind the scenes.

"Lucy, we know you're going to do a great job with the speech. That's why Victoria chose you to be the class speaker. You're going to be amazing," Phoebe declared.

"That's nice of you to say, but that still doesn't change the fact that I'm really nervous." Lucy held the paper she had written her speech on tightly.

Jane sighed. "Okay, we'll listen to it."

"Don't sound so excited," Lucy replied sarcastically.

Phoebe looked at Lucy. "Honestly, just read it already."

Lucy began to recite the speech. "I remember my first day at Minecrafters Academy and how nervous I was—"

Kaboom!

Lucy looked up from the speech and rushed to the window. "What was that?"

"Maybe it was a creeper?" suggested Phoebe.

"It didn't sound like a creeper. It sounded like a TNT explosion." Jane stood next to Lucy, looking out the window and inspecting the campus for smoke.

"I don't see anything." Lucy clutched the speech.

Jane nodded. "I think we should go outside and look around."

Lucy placed the speech in her inventory. She took out her armor and a sword. "We have to be safe."

Her friends agreed, and they put their armor on and grabbed swords from their inventories. They ran down the stairs and into the center of the campus. As they ran out of the building, they spotted Maya and Debbie.

"Maya!" Jane called out.

Maya hurried toward them. "Did you hear that explosion?"

"Yes," Lucy replied. "We were trying to find out where it came from."

"Us, too," Debbie said. She held her diamond sword.

"Let's search together," said Phoebe.

Kaboom!

"Another explosion!" cried Jane.

The gang looked around, but there were no signs of smoke. They were dumbfounded.

"Do you think this is some sort of trick?" asked Maya.

"I don't know. Maybe it's part of a class?" suggested Lucy.

"Or a fireworks display they are practicing for graduation day?" added Debbie.

Lucy looked up at the sky. "It's doubtful that it's a fireworks display. I don't see anything."

The gang walked around the campus. When they reached the Main Hall, Adam called out to them from where he stood next to the entrance, "Over here!" The group ran over to Adam. When they reached him, he told them, "The Overworld is in the middle of an attack. There have been TNT explosions all around the villages and various biomes."

"How do you know?" asked Lucy.

"Our friend from back home, Steve, is here. He says he needs help. Someone has been blowing up houses and shops in our home village. He asked me to leave the academy in order to help them."

"Steve?" Lucy was shocked to hear this news. "Where is he now?"

"He's meeting with Victoria the headmaster. He wants to assemble a team from Minecrafters Academy to help in the battle," explained Adam.

"Who is behind this attack?" asked Debbie.

Adam sighed. "Steve doesn't know, either."

Lucy was upset. It had been a while since the academy and the Overworld had last been under attack. She had been happy during this peaceful period, and now it was about to end. She didn't want to be part of another battle, but she didn't have a choice. If the Overworld was under attack, she would fight to save it.

Phoebe asked, "But what about the explosions we heard on campus?"

"Someone blew up the Great Hall," Adam said and started to walk in the direction of the building.

"The Great Hall!" Lucy gasped.

"But that's a new building!" added Phoebe.

The Great Hall had been designed and constructed by the students of Minecrafters Academy. It had taken them an entire school year to finish the project, and it was where the school had been planning to hold the graduation ceremony.

The group walked across the campus toward the Great Hall. Since it was a new building, it wasn't in the center of the campus like the older buildings. As the friends approached the Great Hall, Lucy could see the side of the building was marred by a large, gaping hole.

"Oh, no!" Lucy cried. "I hope we can fix this before the graduation ceremony. It's only a few days away."

The Great Hall also had a section with rooms for visitors. The group noticed that that portion of the building, in particular, was completely destroyed. Phoebe stood in front of the rubble and asked, "Where are our friends going to stay when they come for graduation?"

Adam shook his head. "This is awful. But I don't think we should worry about graduation when the entire Overworld is under attack."

Lucy knew Adam was right, but she was still upset. They had all worked hard to pass their classes at the academy, and it was disappointing to know they wouldn't have a place to graduate. Lucy was also devastated that building they had spent an entire year designing and constructing had been destroyed by TNT in just a few minutes.

Phoebe walked around the building. "This isn't an easy fix. Whoever did this caused a lot of damage."

Lucy agreed and said, "I'm afraid to see what damage they have caused to the Overworld. I bet Adam and I won't even recognize our village."

Adam said, "We have to help save the Overworld."

As Adam spoke, the group looked across the campus. Steve and Victoria were running toward them.

"We have important news," Victoria called out to the group.

Before they could hear the news, thunder boomed throughout the campus and it began to rain.

A skeleton spawned and shot an arrow at Lucy. "Ouch!" she cried out. Lucy didn't have a moment to fight back. Within seconds a horde of skeletons spawned and shot a barrage of arrows at her, destroying her.

Chapter 2
NEWS FROM THE OVERWORLD

I t was still raining when Lucy respawned in her dorm room. She grabbed a bow and arrow from her inventory and raced to the window to aim at the skeletons.

"Bull's-eye!" she exclaimed as she struck a skeleton with a few arrows, obliterating it.

"Lucy!" Steve rushed into the dorm room.

"Steve, what's going on? Is the academy under another skeleton attack?" Lucy questioned breathlessly as she focused on destroying skeletons with her bow and arrow.

"This is serious. We have to get out of this building, fast," Steve warned her.

"But I can destroy skeletons from my window, and I'll be shielded by the building." Lucy shot another arrow at a skeleton.

Kaboom!

The building shook. Lucy held onto the wall. "Steve, are you okay?"

"Yes." Steve dusted some rubble off of his armor. "But they found tons of TNT all around this building. If we don't get out now, we will be destroyed with this building."

Lucy's voice shook. "And I'll have no place to respawn!"

Steve and Lucy dashed out of the dorm. As they exited the building, there was another explosion. They leapt away from the rubble that fell from the dorms.

"The dorms!" Lucy cried as they ran toward their friends.

"We can rebuild," Steve reassured her. "The important thing is that we got out.

Lucy envied Steve's hopefulness as they raced to battle skeletons in a rainstorm.

Steve looked over at Lucy. "It's going to be alright."

Lucy wasn't sure Steve was right. Two large buildings had been destroyed and the campus was under an intense skeleton attack. They might not be able to rebuild. This could be the battle that could signal the end for Minecrafters Academy and the entire Overworld. But Lucy didn't have time to dwell on this catastrophic thought, because four skeletons surrounded her, forcing her to fight for her life. If they destroyed her, she would respawn in a building that was in the process of falling down. She placed her bow and arrow in her inventory and grabbed her powerful diamond sword instead.

"Ouch!" Lucy cried as two arrows pierced her arm. Lucy grabbed a bottle of milk and took a quick sip to replenish her energy. She struck two skeletons with her diamond sword, but no matter how many times she struck them, the skeletons seemed invulnerable. She couldn't destroy them.

"Help!" Lucy called out. She needed as much help as she could get. Two more arrows landed on her arm, and she was losing hearts.

"I'm here." Maya ran to Lucy's side and struck one of the skeletons with her sword, destroying the bony menace.

Lucy wondered if her sword had lost its power. She wondered if the rain had any affect on the sword's power, because she wasn't able to destroy any skeletons. Lucy was relieved when she finally hit another skeleton and annihilated it. The skeleton dropped arrows, and Lucy reached to pick them up. But while she grabbed the arrows, a skeleton shot an arrow at her.

"Not again!" she cried out in pain, grabbing the remaining milk from her inventory; she took a sip and then struck the skeleton as hard as she could with her diamond sword.

Lucy was beginning to feel confident and struck another skeleton and destroyed it. But everything changed when Lucy saw a bunch of zombies lumbering toward her.

"We have to fight zombies, too!" Lucy gasped.

"We can do it," Maya exclaimed.

Maya ran toward the zombies and slammed them with her sword. Lucy followed Maya and battled the undead mobs. In a moment, Adam and Steve raced over and helped them fight the zombies, too.

"This is awful," Lucy said, exhausted from the battle.

"I know—it's like this all over the Overworld," Steve said as he struck a zombie and destroyed it.

"How long has this been going on?" asked Lucy.

"Not too long, thankfully. The minute the shops in our village were destroyed, I TPed to Minecrafters Academy. I knew we needed help," Steve explained.

Lucy couldn't believe that earlier in the day she had been so focused on the graduation speech. In fact, she had been thinking about nothing but delivering that speech for weeks, now. She had had problems sleeping, and hadn't been able to stop obsessing, imagining making a mistake in front of everyone at the graduation ceremony.

As rain fell on her and she struck zombies and skeletons that attacked her simultaneously, it seemed almost absurd that she had spent so much time worrying about giving a speech. Giving a speech was a lot easier than being destroyed by hostile mobs in the rain and having no place to respawn. Lucy would give a million speeches in front of the largest crowd she could imagine, if this battle would just end.

"Watch out!" Steve called to Lucy.

Lucy turned around and leapt away from a creeper. The arrow that was meant for Lucy pierced the green creeper.

Kaboom!

The creeper exploded and dropped a disc. Lucy reached for the disc. Although she wasn't in the mood for listening to music, she placed the disc in her inventory. She promised herself that she would help win this battle, and when the battle was over, she'd throw an enormous graduation party. Maybe she'd play the disc at it so everyone could dance and celebrate.

Lucy grabbed her arrow and struck the skeleton that destroyed the creeper. As she lunged at the skeleton, the rain stopped and the sky cleared.

Phoebe and Jane walked over to Lucy. Phoebe sipped a potion of healing, then handed it off to Lucy and Jane.

"Thanks," Lucy said as she took a sip. "That was intense."

Her friends agreed. Phoebe added, "I'm sure it's going to get a lot worse, too."

Lucy shrugged. She wanted this to be over. She wanted good news. Lucy turned around when she heard Victoria announce, "Pay attention, everyone. I have important news." Victoria stood in the center of the campus. Stefan, who worked with Victoria, put his head down. He looked upset. The students crowded around them.

Lucy joined the group, wating to hear the important news.

Victoria grimaced as she informed the students, "I'm sorry, but due to circumstances beyond our control we have to cancel graduation."

There was a collective groan among the student body.

Chapter 3
GRADUATION DAY IS CANCELED!

"**B**ut you'll reschedule graduation, right?" someone called out from the crowd.

Victoria stammered, "I'm not sure. We have to see how this battle ends."

The crowd roared. "No graduation?"

"This is awful!"

"No way!"

Seeing the chaos, Victoria looked quickly at Stefan and then called out to the students, "I'm sure we will reschedule. We will win this battle, and we'll celebrate at graduation."

The crowd cheered. "We need to give them hope," Victoria whispered to Stefan. "We can't declare defeat before we start to battle."

The crowd was too fixated on the battle to pay attention to the conversation that was taking place between

Victoria and Stefan. As the crowd's cheers grew louder, a person shouted, "Who are we battling? Do we have any information?"

The crowd quieted as Victoria addressed the question. "We have met with a wheat farmer named Steve. His town is one of the many towns under attack. Unfortunately, we don't know who is behind these attacks."

"Is it Isaac, the old headmaster?" asked another student.

"We don't believe so," said Victoria.

"What about Liam and Dylan? They just attacked the academy," asked another student.

"Liam, Dylan, and Isaac are in the bedrock jail and have no access to the outside world. I'm sure they aren't behind this attack," Victoria declared.

"Well then, who is?" a loud, angry voice asked.

"I don't know. But I'm positive that we will find out who is attacking the Overworld and we'll stop them. This academy has the most skilled fighters in the entire Overworld," said Victoria, and the crowd cheered.

Stefan announced, "We will hold a formal meeting on the lawn after lunch. Everyone, go about your day. We will let you know what the next steps are in a couple of hours."

Lucy couldn't believe Stefan expected them to just go about their day. How could they just act as if nothing was happening? The Overworld was under attack, and graduation had been canceled.

"I want to get lunch," Phoebe admitted, "but I'm afraid the building is going to explode."

"I'm sure they wouldn't let us eat in the dining hall unless they had already inspected the entire building for TNT," Jane told her friend.

Steve joined Lucy and her friends as they walked toward the dining hall. They grabbed trays and filled them with food.

Lucy put more and more food on her tray until it was almost overflowing. "You guys, you should get more food than that," she said. "I'm placing a lot of this food in my inventory. You never know when we we'll have access to food. We have no idea where we will be sent in the Overworld. This is war."

Lucy's friends went back to the buffet and filled their trays. They knew Lucy was right; they had to be prepared for the battle.

As they ate the food, Stefan approached their table. "Steve, it's nice to have you join us for lunch. I want everyone at this table to work together as a team."

Steve asked, "Will they join me on the journey back to the wheat farm?"

"Yes," Stefan replied. "You don't have to stay for the meeting. You can go straight to the wheat farm after lunch. I have a feeling that you'll not only save your village, Steve, but these skilled warriors will also help discover who is behind this evil attack."

Lucy was excited to return to the wheat farm and the village she had come from, but she was also scared to see how badly it was damaged. Lucy loved the town and she felt like it was her home, no matter how much time she'd spent at the academy. If she saw Steve's farmhouse destroyed or the village streets filled with rubble, she feared she'd get too emotional and it would impact her fighting skills. Tears rolled down Lucy's face, just at the thought.

"Are you okay?" Phoebe asked Lucy.

"Yes," she replied. "I'm just heartbroken that the village has been attacked and the Overworld will be in shambles."

"But we're going to fix it." Phoebe smiled.

Lucy wanted to be like the others. She wanted to be more confident and believe they would win, but she had to admit that she was nervous for the battle. She took her final bite from her apple and announced, "I'm ready to go. Are you guys?"

Her friends nodded. They were ready to embark on their journey to Steve's wheat farm.

As they exited the dining hall, the lights went out.

"Oh no! Another attack!" cried Jane.

"Does anybody have a torch?" asked Adam.

Before they could reach for their torches, a loud explosion startled them.

Kaboom!

Smoke filled the room, and nobody could see. But then, without warning, the lights turned back on.

"That was odd," remarked Adam. "There wasn't even a hostile mob invasion."

"Yes," Lucy agreed. "But what exploded? I don't see any damage to the dining hall."

The group looked around. Phoebe walked outside the dining hall and called out, "It looks like someone exploded blocks of TNT in the basement."

Everyone crowded around the entrance to the basement. Smoke filled the staircase.

"I don't think we should go down there." Phoebe held her hand in front of her face to shield herself from the smoke.

Adam looked at the gang. "We should go."

Lucy agreed and then asked, "Where's Steve?"

The gang called Steve's name and walked around the building, but there was no reply.

Chapter 4
OLD FEARS

"Steve!" Lucy called out again, but there was no response.

"Do you think he's in the basement?" Phoebe looked down the smoke filled stairs.

"If he went down there, he has to have been destroyed by the explosion," Adam said sadly.

"Do you think he respawned on the wheat farm and will TP back here?" Lucy questioned.

Nobody knew the answer to that. They looked around at each other in shock.

Stefan walked toward the group. "You need to get going. You have to help save the Overworld."

"But Steve is missing," Maya informed him.

"Steve?" Stefan raised his voice. "Missing?"

"Yes. After the lights went on, he was gone." Lucy was so upset that she could barely get the words out.

"How?" Stefan began to pace.

Victoria walked out of the dining hall. "Is everything okay?"

"Steve is missing," Stefan told her the awful news.

"We have to find him," Victoria announced.

Everyone had a plan. Lucy wanted to stay on the campus and search for Steve. Adam thought they should head to the wheat farm. Jane wanted to assemble a larger team to help them battle in the Overworld, because she thought they needed more backup.

While the discussions intensified, a man wearing a green hat and a purple cape and carrying a shield spawned in front of them. He shouted at the group.

"Silence! Your friend Steve is now my prisoner. And soon I'll be the ruler of the Overworld." He laughed.

Lucy was shaking as she asked, "Who are you?"

Phoebe screamed, "Where's Steve?"

"I'm your worst enemy." He laughed and splashed a potion on himself and disappeared.

The group was terrified. Victoria said, "Now we know who is behind this attack. We can defeat him."

Everyone cheered, but it sounded halfhearted.

Stefan looked over at Lucy. "I think you should still travel back to the wheat farm. I promised Steve that we would help save his town."

Lucy nodded, and her friends followed her reluctantly. As they walked off the Minecrafters Academy campus, Lucy paused and looked up at the large mountain they had to climb to reach Steve's village. She took a deep breath.

When they reached the top of the mountain, Phoebe paused. "Can we see Steve's village from here?" she asked.

"No," Lucy replied and showed Phoebe the town on map. "It's a long journey from here."

Lucy recalled taking the journey to Minecrafters Academy with Steve and their friends, Henry and Max. It seemed so long ago, now. She had been excited to be with her good friends, but nervous to start at a new school. Now she was terrified about traveling back to the village, because she couldn't bear to see the village destroyed.

Adam told the others, "I used to live in Steve's village. I know it well. I'll be glad to reunite with old friends and help them fight this evil villain."

The sun was setting, and Maya suggested they build a shelter before nightfall. "We can build one here," she said, pointing to a patch of grass outside of the swampy biome.

"Do you think we can make it through the swampy biome and then build a house?" asked Lucy. "I don't want any witches or slimes attacking us."

"I think we're far enough from the swamp that we shouldn't have to worry about an attack from a witch," Maya said as she began to pull wooden planks and other supplies out from her inventory.

As the gang constructed a house, Lucy could see a bat flying in the distance. She really didn't want to spend the night near the swamp.

"Do you hear a noise?" Lucy asked as she placed a window on the house.

"No, I don't hear anything." Phoebe was annoyed. She was trying to finish the house before dark and she didn't want to be distracted.

Boing! Boing! Boing!

"Shh!" Lucy said to her friends. "Don't you hear that noise? It sounds like slimes."

Nobody heard the noise. Lucy felt like she was going crazy. How could she be the only one who heard the bouncing noise?

As Jane placed the door on the house and Adam took out a torch from his inventory to put next to the door, Lucy screamed, "Slimes!"

"She's right!" Maya cried as a group of six boxy slimes bounced toward them.

Phoebe suggested that they hide in the house, but Jane called out, "No! We must destroy them."

Lucy leapt at the slimes and pierced a gelatinous creature with her diamond sword. The slimy mob broke into smaller blocks. Debbie helped Lucy destroy the little slimes that bounced toward them.

"Thanks," Lucy said as they defeated the final mini slime.

"Over here," cried Phoebe. "Help us!"

Lucy looked up to see Phoebe and Jane surrounded by too many slimes to count. "We can't get destroyed on this trip! Help!" Jane's voice shook.

They were right. The dorms were a pile of rubble, and that meant if anyone was destroyed before they slept somewhere else, they'd have no place to respawn. They had to spend the night in this house in the swamp. Lucy and Debbie sprinted toward their friends and struck the boxy slimes.

Adam and Maya were battling their own group of slimes when they heard a whimper.

"I hear someone crying," Maya called out.

Lucy was obliterating the final slime as she heard the cries. "I hear the same thing you do," she told Maya.

Once the final slime was destroyed, the group ran toward the sound of the cries. The sky was getting darker and the group worried they would be attacked by hostile mobs that spawned at night. They were vulnerable, but they knew they had to find out who was crying and try to help them.

"It sounds like it's coming from in here." Adam pointed to a small cave outside of the swampy biome.

"I don't think we should go in the cave. I'm pretty sure that's where the slimes are coming from," said Lucy.

"But can't you hear the cries?" asked Maya. "We have to go in."

"I hope this isn't a trap," Lucy said as she followed her friends into the darkness.

Adam took out another torch and placed it on the wall of the cave.

"Hello?" Lucy shouted. "We're here to help you."

"Lucy!" a familiar voice called out.

Chapter 5
SMALL PESTS

"Steve!" Lucy sprinted to her friend. "We have to get you out of here quickly."

Weakly, Steve whispered, "Watch out. This is a trap."

Before they could help Steve escape, the man in the green hat and purple cape appeared in front of them.

"Now you're all my prisoners." He laughed.

"Never!" Lucy shouted as she leapt toward the man with her diamond sword. He splashed a potion of weakness on Lucy, and she started to lose hearts.

"You don't want to get destroyed. Where will you respawn, Lucy?" he asked, laughing.

Lucy stood frozen in terror. She didn't know how he knew her name. The caped criminal walked closer to Lucy. She cried, "Leave me alone."

Adam ran to Lucy and handed her milk. "Drink this." Adam threw a potion of harming on the caped villain.

The man was weakened. "You won't get away with this, Adam."

Phoebe, Jane, Maya, and Debbie ran toward the caped man, striking him with their diamond swords. He was powerful, but he was overwhelmed, and they were able to destroy him.

Adam gave Steve a potion of healing. "You need to get your strength back," he said. "We have a place for you to sleep tonight."

As the group tried to leave the cave, silverfish that were crawling on the floor bit them.

"Look down!" Phoebe shrieked.

The ground of the cave was carpeted in silverfish. The group used their swords to destroy the mobs, but it was pointless. There were too many to fight.

"We have to get out of here. This is a trap!" Steve called to his friends.

"What about the silverfish? We have to destroy them. They're attacking us." Lucy slammed her sword into a large group of silverfish.

"I'm telling you, we have to forget about destroying the silverfish. This is a trap. That man will be back. He's a terrible, evil person," Steve said.

But a voice interrupted him, "It's so nice to hear such kind words spoken about me." The caped man pointed his diamond sword at Steve.

Lucy rushed toward the man and struck him with her diamond sword, but she couldn't fight him for very long. She had too many silverfish biting her feet, and they were depleting her energy. She had very few hearts left.

Adam called out to his friends, "Sprint to me!"

The group hurried toward Adam and he splashed a potion of invisibility of them. Getting the potion on his friends wasn't an easy job, and Adam narrowly avoided splashing the potion on the man in the green hat, too. When everyone was invisible, they ran toward the house.

"Is everyone here?" Adam asked as they entered the house.

"I'm here!" Lucy called out. They did an informal roll call, and everyone was in the house.

They hadn't crafted beds yet, and it was hard to do so while they were invisible. Everyone kept bumping into each other. But soon, the house was filled with beds and everyone became visible.

Lucy noticed something crawling on the floor. "Is that a silverfish?"

Adam grabbed his sword and went to strike the small insect. But as he hit the bug, he said, "No! I It's an endermite."

"Did someone leave the door open?" Phoebe asked as she walked to the door, but it was closed.

"More endermites!" Steve called out and went to strike the pesky insects.

"I'm sure that man is behind this," Lucy called out as she destroyed another endermite.

"Is there a spawner?" Debbie cried.

"I don't see one." Adam searched the ground.

Jane looked out the window and saw two pairs of purple eyes staring at her. Then she heard a loud shriek.

"I'm going to be attacked by Endermen!" Jane's heart was pounding. She was terrified.

Lucy dashed toward the door. She opened it and raced alongside Jane. "There's water near the swamp biome," Lucy said. "Don't worry, Jane. We'll get you to the water."

Jane ran as fast as she could. She didn't want to turn around because she feared the Endermen would destroy her. As the lanky beasts reached for Jane, she jumped into the cloudy swamp water. "Yuck!" she called out, and the Endermen followed her into the water.

Jane rinsed the dirty swamp water off her body before running back to the house. When she walked to the door, she was relieved to hear Maya call out, "I think I destroyed the final endermite."

"Great. We have to get to bed." Steve sounded exhausted.

When Lucy finally got into her bed, she sighed. "What a crazy day."

Adam said, "I'm so glad that we have Steve back with us."

"I'm happy to be back with you, too." Steve explained how he was trapped by the caped man. "He threw a potion of weakness on me when the lights were off. I didn't even know what was happening. He then made me TP to that cave, where we met some of the evil people who are working on destroying the Overworld with him."

"Who are they?" asked Phoebe.

"He covered up my eyes, so I couldn't see them, and could only hear their voices," said Steve.

"We have to get to sleep," Lucy warned the others. "If we don't, we'll be extremely vulnerable. We need a place to respawn."

The gang agreed. They needed to have a spot where they could all respawn if the caped man returned or a hostile mob destroyed them. Lucy pulled the covers over herself and began to drift off to sleep.

In the morning, Lucy crawled out of bed and walked toward the window. The sun was shining, making it a great day to travel to the wheat farm—if only their mission weren't so desperate. The gang sat and ate apples, gathering their strength for the journey.

"Are you ready?" Steve asked the others, and he led them toward the wheat farm. They were halfway there when Phoebe called out, "Ouch!" as an arrow pierced her arm.

They looked around, but they couldn't see where the arrow came from.

"Ow!" cried Maya. An arrow hit her hand.

"Who's there?" screamed Lucy.

There was no reply. Adam said, "Let's keep going. We don't want anything to stop us. We're almost there."

As the gang continued their journey, they kept a close eye out for arrows that might be flying in their direction. As they reached the grassy biome outside of Steve's village, Debbie cried in pain.

"I've been struck by an arrow," she moaned.

The purple-caped man sprinted toward them. He grinned and taunted them, "Guess who?"

Chapter 6
VILLAGERS

Adam splashed a potion of harming on the caped man. The man used his last bit of energy to strike Adam, but he couldn't stop Adam from splashing a second potion of harming on him.

"I'm losing hearts!" the man cried out.

Lucy struck the man with her diamond sword and he lost more hearts. Phoebe shot an arrow at him. The man tried to run but he tripped and fell into the water. As he stood up in the shallow water, Phoebe shot another arrow at him, destroying the caped criminal.

"We have to get to my village," Steve exclaimed.

The gang left the grassy biome and raced to the village. Adam smiled when they spotted the iron golem in the distance.

"Look, it's the golem! We're home!" Adam looked over at Steve.

Steve stopped. "We should come up with a plan before we enter the village. Once we show up, everyone is going to ask what we can do to help."

Kaboom!

Smoke rose from the village, and Lucy's heart raced. She didn't want to see the village destroyed.

"Steve," said Lucy. "I don't think we have time to come up with a plan. We have to save the village and stop the caped griefer. That's the only plan."

Steve agreed. "We have to find out what exploded." He raced toward the village and the others followed.

As they entered the village, Lucy was shocked to see that the shops were open. The library, the church, and the blacksmith shop were all intact. Eliot the Blacksmith saw Steve and his friends. He left his shop and greeted them.

"Lucy!" Eliot was happy to be reunited with his old friend. "You're back! And Adam, too! What a pleasant surprise."

Lucy smiled. "I'm so happy to see you, Eliot. I just wish it was under better circumstances."

"I feel the same way," added Adam.

Lucy introduced Eliot to her friends, Phoebe, Jane, Maya, and Debbie.

"I'm happy you assembled a team, Steve. This will be very helpful," Eliot remarked.

Steve questioned Eliot, "What has happened since I left? We just heard an explosion. Do you know what exploded? Has a man wearing a cape terrorized the people and the villagers? Are there random attacks from hostile mobs?"

"Slow down, Steve." Eliot smiled. "That was too many questions. We've been lucky. Things have been quiet since you left. The explosion you just heard came from Kyra's house. She has been constructing and testing different booby traps to help protect us from the evil griefer who is attacking the Overworld."

"You know about the caped griefer?" asked Steve.

"We didn't know he wore a cape. But we know the Overworld is under attack and it's the work of a griefer. We've been through this before. Kyra was trying to help protect us."

"We need to see Kyra," Steve told Eliot, and the gang rushed to Kyra's house.

Steve let out a sigh of relief when he passed his wheat farm and saw that the farmhouse was still intact. They knocked on the door of his neighbor, Kyra's, home.

"Steve! Lucy! Adam!" Kyra exclaimed, coming around the house from the backyard. "I'm so glad you're here!"

Lucy introduced Kyra to her new friends.

"This is fantastic," said Kyra. "We are going to need all the help we can get."

"Great. We want to help." Phoebe smiled at Kyra.

"Follow me." Kyra waved for the friends to follow her and led them into her large backyard, which was strewn with booby traps.

As they walked around the yard, Steve remarked, "Eliot said things have been quiet here."

"Yes, but I know we're about to be attacked. People from various towns have been arriving here each day. They are refugees. They had to leave their towns and villages because they were destroyed or are currently under attack from the griefer army."

"How do you know the village is about to be attacked?" asked Jane.

"If everyone else's village was destroyed, ours has to be next."

Lucy blurted out, "We met the griefer. He wears a green hat, a purple cape, and a shield."

Lucy was thinking about other traits she could describe that would help Kyra identify the griefer, but then they heard another explosion.

"Oh no!" Kyra cried. "That definitely didn't come from me. We are under attack!"

The gang ran out of Kyra's house, but they didn't get past the front garden. A sea of arrows flew at them. Lucy tried to dodge one of the arrows, but it hit her unarmored leg.

"Ouch!" she cried as she looked up at the caped man and his army of men dressed in jeans, grey T-shirts, and wings. Some of the soldiers were flying above them.

The caped griefer laughed. "We're going to destroy your town."

Kyra screamed, "Never!" She called to her friends, "Follow me!"

The group followed Kyra back to her house, swerving and dodging to avoid the many arrows the griefers were shooting at them.

"I can't believe these griefers can fly." Jane stared at a winged man who flew above them.

"It looks like they are gliding," remarked Maya.

"It looks like they are going to be really hard to fight," added Jane.

Adam shot an arrow at one of the winged griefers and the griefer fell to the ground. But another glided down and flung an arrow at Lucy's head.

"Oh no!" Lucy cried out as the arrow hit her.

"Lucy!" Phoebe called, sprinting to her side. "Take this milk."

Lucy sipped milk as she followed Kyra, who raced toward her home "We have to lead them into my house," she called. "I'm going to blow it up with TNT."

"But we'll be in the house with them!" Lucy was confused.

"No, we won't. I built a stronghold underneath my house." Kyra opened the door and led them to the stronghold.

The caped griefer ran toward the house and hollered, "You can't hide in there." He ordered his soldiers to break down the door.

"They aren't here!" one of the soldiers called to the caped man, searching the house.

"What? That's impossible." He went inside to investigate.

Kaboom!

Chapter 7
MYSTERY IN THE MINE

Kyra led the group down a dimly lit tunnel made of dirt. Phoebe grabbed a torch from her inventory and placed it on the wall.

"This is quite a large stronghold," Phoebe said and then asked, "You built this place yourself?"

"Most of it was constructed by another griefer. I just dug a tunnel from my house and opened it up," Kyra said. "It had been closed for years."

Lucy remembered when Henry had been trapped in this stronghold and they had spent days searching for him. Now they were using the same tunnels that had trapped their friend to escape a new enemy. Lucy wondered where in the Overworld her treasure-hunting friends, Max and Henry, were. She hoped they weren't being destroyed by this griefer invasion.

"Watch out!" Maya shrieked.

Cave spiders emerged from a room in the stronghold and crawled toward them.

Lucy struck one of them with her sword. "At least it's not silverfish."

Everyone agreed.

"Is there a way out of here?" asked Debbie.

"Yes, follow me. If we walk down this tunnel. . . ." Kyra paused and pointed out a light peeking through a long tunnel. "We can crawl through a hole that leads into Valentino's butcher shop."

The gang walked down the long hall, watching the ground for cave spiders and silverfish. Lucy was surprised when she heard voices coming from the opposite direction. She stopped.

"Does anyone hear those voices?" she asked.

Steve replied, "Yes. Do you think the griefers made it down here?"

"I'm not sure, but we should see who is down here with us," suggested Lucy.

Jane's voice shook. "Let's just get out of here."

Kyra announced, "It sounds like the voices are coming from the mine."

"The mine?" Steve asked.

Lucy and Kyra walked toward the mine. The voices grew louder. Lucy said, "There's definitely someone in the mine."

Everyone took out their diamond swords, ready for battle.

Lucy peeked in the room and saw two people mining. They looked familiar. "Henry? Max?"

Henry's hands were filled with diamonds. "Lucy! It's so great seeing you here. We just arrived in town. We went to Steve's house, but he wasn't there."

"We tried to hide in Kyra's house but it had exploded," Max interrupted. "There was a hole in the center of the ground where her house once stood, and it took us to this incredible, treasure-filled mine. Do you see the diamonds?" Max showed Lucy his diamonds.

Henry placed his diamonds in his inventory. "Why are you here? Aren't you supposed to be at Minecrafters Academy? Max and I are all set to go to your graduation next week."

"I'm looking forward to hearing your speech," said Max enthusiastically as he placed the rest of his diamonds in his inventory.

"There is no graduation," Lucy said with a frown. "It was cancelled. The Overworld is under attack, and most of our campus has been destroyed." Lucy's eyes welled with tears.

"Oh, Lucy, that's awful," said Max. "I knew a griefer was attacking the Overworld, but I didn't know it was that bad."

"It is," Lucy cried. "And it looks like they're back!"

"Ugh!" Steve screamed as two arrows struck his arm.

A laugh boomed throughout the enclosed space. Then a voice yelled, "Game over!"

Lucy fled toward the entrance to the mine and gasped. There were hundreds of winged griefers in the stronghold. The ones who didn't have wings carried shields. Lucy could barely move. All of the soldiers aimed their bow and arrows at her. Lucy closed her eyes and took a deep breath.

Lucy was actually relieved to respawn in the small house outside the swamp. She sat up in the bed and grabbed an apple from her inventory, waiting for the others to respawn. As she chewed her apple, she grew impatient.

"How could they survive that battle?" she asked herself.

Lucy paced around the small house. She walked outside. The sky was growing dark. Two bats flew in the distance, and in the sky the moon was full. She decided to TP to her friends.

But before she TPed, she heard someone call out her name, and Maya walked out of the house.

Lucy smiled and raced toward Maya. "I'm so glad you're here. How are the others?"

"Not good. The caped man took everyone prisoner," Maya explained. "I was accidently destroyed when a silverfish bit me."

Lucy gave Maya an apple. "Take this. You're still weak."

"Thanks," said Maya. "You can't believe what this evil griefer is making our friends do for him. He forced them all to place bricks of TNT around Eliot's blacksmith shop and Valentino's butcher shop, and he is making them blow up the shops."

"How could he do that? Those shops are vital to the town's survival, and Eliot and Valentino are my good friends. I don't want to see those shops destroyed."

"I told you, this is a very serious battle." Maya finished the apple.

"We need to TP back to our friends, right now!" Lucy exclaimed.

Lucy and Maya TPed, but they arrived in the center of the village too late. The minute they arrived, there was a loud explosion.

Kaboom!

"No!" Valentino's cries rang throughout the village.

Lucy hurried over to Valentino's side to comfort him. "I'm so sorry about your shop."

Valentino was devastated. "How can Steve do this to me? He's my friend. Steve is always in my shop."

Eliot ran to Valentino's side. "Steve also destroyed my blacksmith shop! I thought he was one of my best friends."

"It's not his fault," Lucy said.

But Eliot the blacksmith and Valentino the butcher didn't believe her.

"Lucy," Valentino explained, "I saw it with my own eyes. Steve is a griefer."

A townsperson walking past them overheard Valentino. She stopped. "Did I hear you say that Steve is the griefer?"

"Yes," Eliot nodded his head.

The townsperson raced through town screaming, "We found the griefer. It's Steve!"

Townspeople ran from their homes, shouting in unison, "Steve is a griefer!"

Lucy was terrified. Maya called out, "It's not Steve!"

Nobody listened. A gang of villagers and townspeople sprinted into the center of town, enraged.

Just at that moment, Steve stumbled into town, looking disoriented. The villagers immediately charged.

"Help!" Steve yelled.

All Lucy could hear was the roar of the angry crowd that surrounded Steve, as one of the townspeople aimed his bow and arrow and screamed, "You're going to pay for this!" The crowd drowned out Steve's cries for help.

"He's innocent!" Lucy called to the angry mob, but nobody listened.

Jane walked into town and stood next to Steve, her bow and arrow at the ready. She shot an arrow at a townsperson. "Listen up! Steve isn't the griefer."

When the arrow pierced the townsperson, the crowd directed their attention to Jane.

"Why are you attacking us?" the townsperson asked.

"Because I'm trying to tell you that Steve is innocent."

"Then why did he blow up Valentino's butcher shop and Eliot's blacksmith shop?" questioned the crowd.

"The real griefers forced him to do it," Jane told them.

"Who are the real griefers?" asked a townsperson.

"There's a man wearing a purple cape and a green hat," she stammered. "He has an army of winged men."

"Where are they?" demanded the townsperson.

"They've disappeared," she replied. "They took us prisoner, but then they let us go."

"We don't believe you!" a villager cried out.

"Attack Steve!" cried another.

Steve was helpless as a large, angry crowd sprinted toward him.

Chapter 8
TNT

Lucy felt helpless. She had to save Steve, but she didn't know how to do it. She grabbed a brick of TNT and placed it where it wouldn't hurt anyone. Then, she ignited it.

Kaboom!

The explosion rocked the village.

"Another griefer!" one of the townspeople cried.

"No, I'm not," Lucy defended herself. "I just wanted to get your attention. You are focusing on the wrong people. There is an evil, caped man, and he is taking over the Overworld. You have to help us stop him."

"Nonsense!" a townsperson cried.

A group of townspeople sprinted toward Lucy. "Get her!" one of them shouted.

Lucy's heart was beating fast. "Help!" she cried to her friends.

"You have the wrong people," a voice called out from the entrance to town.

Everyone stopped and stared at the caped man. He stood by the iron golem. "I'm going to destroy this golem, and then I will spawn zombies to attack your town. As I told your friend Steve, the game is over. I am in control of the Overworld."

A townsperson gasped. "Steve was telling the truth."

Another townsperson exclaimed, "There really is caped criminal."

"Yes," the man in the cape announced. "I am your worst enemy. I can't believe you thought Steve was behind this attack. You don't trust your own friend? Hasn't Steve been protecting your village?"

The caped man walked over to Steve. "How can you ever befriend these villagers and townspeople? Look how quickly they turned against you?"

Steve stood silently, looking between the griefer and the friends who had just attacked him.

Valentino rushed over and tried to explain. "But, we saw you with the TNT, Steve. We thought you were the griefer."

"I knew if I forced Steve to destroy your little shop, you'd believe he was evil. You're so easy to manipulate." The man in the green hat and purple cape laughed loudly. "This is why I don't have any friends, just people who work for me."

The man summoned his army. One of the soldiers asked, "What do you want me to do, boss?"

"Destroy that iron golem," he ordered.

The soldiers rushed to the iron golem and destroyed it.

"Good job!" the man commended his minions.

"What next?" asked another soldier.

"I want you to destroy this town with TNT. Obliterate it. I want nothing left of it." He laughed again.

But as the evil man laughed, the sound was drowned out by thunder, and rain began to pour down. Lucy noticed that the caped criminal looked confused.

"Look, boss. There are zombies," a soldier pointed out.

The sky grew darker, as if someone was manipulating the weather and the time. Endermen walked past them as skeletons spawned.

"Endermen!" a soldier called out. "How?"

"Don't stare at them!" the caped man informed his soldiers.

An Enderman shrieked and teleported to the soldier. Lucy's first instinct was to help the soldier and lead him to the large body of water that was right outside the village, but she knew that he was the enemy and she shouldn't help him.

Skeletons shot arrows at the townspeople and the soldiers. The caped man demanded, "Everyone, fight. Use your skills!"

Lucy looked around and noticed that she and her friends were fighting this battle alongside the griefers. This could only mean one thing: someone else attacking the Overworld.

The caped man was angry as he battled a zombie and an Enderman. "Help me," he called out.

Lucy was battling skeletons. Jane and Phoebe joined Lucy in battle. Jane pointed out, "This appears to be the work of another griefer."

"I know," Lucy agreed. "I think we have a bigger battle on our hands than we imagined."

Zombies lumbered through the town, ripping doors off their hinges and turning villagers into zombie villagers.

Steve ran to Lucy. "I hope you have a lot of golden apples in your inventory. We're going to need them to help these villagers."

Phoebe was shocked. "You're going to help the villagers? After they were so quick to try to destroy you?"

"They didn't believe you, Steve," Jane added.

"I know, but I can't let them be destroyed by zombies. They are helpless. And you can't blame them. They saw me blow up Valentino and Eliot's shops."

Eliot and Valentino ran over to Steve, fending off their enemies long enough to apologize.

"This is no time for apologies," declared Steve. "We have to defeat the real enemy."

Two block-carrying Endermen walked toward the Steve and his friends.

Lucy accidently made eye contact with one of the lanky mobs. "It's going to attack me!" she cried out.

She dashed to the water. She didn't want to look back at the battle. Lucy jumped into the water. She was relieved to see the Endermen follow her into the ocean and get destroyed.

The water was refreshing, and Lucy wanted to escape into the deep blue ocean, but she knew she couldn't abandon her friends. She had to drag herself out of the water and into the battle.

She rushed toward the village, but stopped and looked up when she heard a loud roar. It was the Ender Dragon.

Chapter 9
IS THIS THE END?

"The Ender Dragon!" the man in the purple cape screamed as the dragon lunged at him. Its scaly wing struck him.

Lucy saw the caped villain was growing weaker, and she sprinted toward him with her diamond sword. She slammed her sword against the side of the dragon and then struck the man in the cape.

"Stop!" he cried out, but Lucy didn't listen. With a last blow from hersword, she destroyed the man.

His soldiers were horrified and ran toward Lucy, ready to attack. Before they could reach her, the Ender Dragon flew into the group of soldiers, destroying them.

Lucy could see the dragon flying right toward her. She tried to avoid being struck by the dragon by running into the library. Avery the Librarian was hiding behind a stack of books.

"Lucy," Avery called out, "there are zombies in the library. Watch out!"

Four vacant-eyed zombies were knocking down bookshelves. Lucy hid behind a shelf and aimed her bow and arrow at the zombies, striking two of them, but the zombies spotted her. She grabbed a potion of invisibility and splashed it on herself. Once she was invisible, she traded her bow and arrow for a sword and rushed over to the zombies.

"I got them!" she told Avery.

"Where are you?" Avery asked.

"I'm over here. Listen to the sound of my voice and you'll find me," Lucy told her friend.

As Avery listened for Lucy's voice, the side of the library began to crumble.

"The library has been struck by the Ender Dragon," Lucy cried. "Avery, be careful."

The dragon's tail was stuck in the wall, and Lucy took the opportunity to hit the tail with an arrow. The dragon lost a heart, and an instant later there was a loud explosion.

Phoebe and Jane fled into the library. "Lucy!" Jane called out. "The Ender Dragon has been destroyed!"

"Were you the one who defeated the Ender Dragon?" asked Phoebe.

Phoebe and Jane couldn't spot Lucy in the library.

"Lucy!" Jane called out. "Where are you?"

"I'm here." Lucy began to reappear, and she asked, "Was I the one who defeated the Ender Dragon? I just struck the tail. It must have been very weak."

"But the griefers took out its wings," said Jane.

Adam opened the door to the library. Lucy could see sunlight coming through the door. "Has the rain ended?" she asked.

"Yes," Adam replied, "and the soldiers are gone. We destroyed them all."

Lucy raced outside. A portal to the End had spawned in the center of town.

"Don't even think about going to the End, Lucy." Maya stood next to her. "We need you here. We have to find out who was behind that hostile mob attack, and who spawned the Ender Dragon."

"I think we are fight two enemies," Lucy said grimly. She couldn't believe there were two sets of griefers terrorizing the Overworld.

Lucy didn't travel to the End, but stayed in the village and inspected the damage done by the Ender Dragon and the griefers serving the caped man. She spotted Steve standing in front of Valentino's shop.

"I can't believe I let them force me to destroy Valentino's shop," Steve said.

Lucy reassured her friend. "This wasn't your fault. We are going to destroy those griefers and find out who is behind the other attack."

Valentino and Eliot approached Steve. "We're so sorry that we blamed you for this damage."

The townspeople and villagers joined Valentino and Eliot and apologized to Steve. A townsperson said, "We will always believe you from now on, Steve."

"It's okay," Steve replied. "But we need all the townspeople to help us battle this enemy."

Lucy announced, "We need to assemble everyone. There are two enemies that need to be destroyed: the caped griefer and his winged hooligans, and an unknown enemy who spawned this hostile Ender Dragon invasion."

Lucy stopped talking when she saw Victoria and Stefan walk into town.

"Stefan! Victoria! What are you doing here?" Phoebe raced toward the folks from Minecrafters Academy.

"We need your help," Victoria said weakly.

"What happened?" asked Maya.

"The attacks on the academy have gotten worse in the last few days. There are hardly any buildings left," explained Victoria.

"And it gets worse," Stefan said. He looked distraught.

"Liam and Dylan have escaped," Victoria confessed.

"That's probably who is behind this last attack!" Lucy exclaimed.

"Now we know our other enemy!" Phoebe nodded and then asked, "What about Isaac?"

"Isaac is still on campus. He is trying to help protect the school," said Victoria.

"What do you want us to do?" asked Lucy.

Victoria replied, "We've heard from some of our students that Liam and Dylan have taken over the cold taiga biome. They built a headquarters on the side of a snow-covered mountain, and they are planning all sorts of attacks."

"That's awful." Lucy shook her head.

"We need you guys to destroy the headquarters," Victoria said matter-of-factly.

Lucy's jaw dropped. She wasn't sure how they would destroy the headquarters, and she was shocked that Victoria had such faith in them.She wasn't even sure she wanted to travel to the cold taiga biome, especially when Steve's village was in jeopardy of being destroyed.

"We will do it," Maya told Victoria.

"Do we all have to go?" Lucy asked. She looked at her group of friends.

"I'm afraid so," Stefan answered. "This is a big job, and we need a lot of help."

"Will you be joining us?" Jane asked Victoria and Stefan.

"Yes, we will," said Victoria. "And we have to leave right now."

Chapter 10
COLD JOURNEY

"**W**ho will protect our village if the flying grief-ers come back?" one of the townspeople asked. The others crowded around her, looking worried.

"You will," Steve explained, putting a reassuring hand on the townsperson's shoulder. "But everyone has to stick together and trust each other."

Lucy added, "We must go to the cold biome and stop Liam and Dylan. They were the ones that who spawned the Ender Dragon."

Kyra suggested, "Why don't Henry, Max, and I stay to help protect the village?"

Lucy knew that was a great plan, but she was heartbroken to leave her good friends just after having been reunited. Still, she smiled at them. "We'll see you soon."

While Kyra, Henry, Max, and the townspeople held a meeting and set up teams to protect different sections of the village, the rest of the gang started their journey to the cold taiga biome.

Victoria held a map in her hands. "This will lead us to Liam and Dylan. We have to travel along the shoreline. Once we spot a large mountain, the cold biome is on the other side."

"At least we can stock up on snowballs, in case we have to battle any Nether mobs or we are attacked by the Ender Dragon again." Phoebe tried to see the bright side of things.

"I guess so." Lucy paused. "I'm not a fan of the cold biome. And I don't want to battle Liam and Dylan again. They are ruthless fighters."

The battle with Liam and Dylan was still fresh on everyone's mind. As they walked along the shoreline, Stefan warned them, "I see something up ahead. It looks like caped man."

"I see him, too," Steve whispered.

"Get your weapons out," Maya informed her friends. "We have to be prepared."

The group doused themselves in their potions of invisibility and crept toward the caped man and his army of winged and shield-carrying soldiers.

The caped man with the shield was on the ground. As they watched, he placed soul sand in a T shape. The gang knew that he was summoning the Wither. The caped leader placed Wither skulls on the soul sand and, within seconds, there was an explosion. The blue Wither spawned and knocked down a small house that stood next to a tree. The caped man stood and turned to look for the friends he planned to attack.

A winged soldier called out, "They're gone!"

"What do you mean, they're gone?" The caped criminal was annoyed.

"They must have stopped and turned around." The winged soldier glided higher, but he couldn't see the gang.

"That's impossible," the man replied.

"What are we going to do about the Wither?" a soldier asked as he dodged Wither skulls.

The Wither flew toward the caped leader. He leapt at the Wither with his diamond sword and struck the flying beast.

"We have to build a bedrock structure to trap him," the man called out as he struck the Wither again.

The Wither spotted the gang. This incredibly powerful hostile mob could see people who were invisible to the naked eye.

Lucy's heart raced. "I think the Wither saw us," she whispered.

"That's fine," Phoebe said. "As long as the winged soldiers can't see us, we might be able to defeat this flying devil."

Wither skulls flew in their direction, and the gang narrowly avoided being hit. The caped man noticed the Wither flying away.

"I think we're not alone," he said with a laugh. He sounded relieved. He didn't want the Wither to destroy his people. He wanted it to annihilate Lucy and her friends.

Lucy sprinted toward the Wither and struck it with her diamond sword. The Wither was losing hearts.

"It's weakened," she called to her friends. "We have to keep hitting it."

As the gang repeatedly struck the Wither, the caped man ordered his soldiers to stop crafting a bedrock trap. "Although I can't see our real enemy, I can see that the Wither is attacking them." He let out a boisterous laugh.

Lucy struck the Wither again. The three-headed beast cried out in pain and then exploded, dropping a Nether star. Lucy picked up the Nether star and placed it in her inventory.

"I can see you!" Jane called out to her friend.

"Good job destroying the Wither!" Phoebe exclaimed.

"Yes, good job," the caped man cried as he ran toward Lucy, clutching a potion of harming.

Steve aimed his bow and arrow at the caped man and it struck his arm. The man called out, "You're not going to stop me."

Lucy tried to shield herself from the potion of harming, but it was too late; the caped man had splashed the potion on her body. She was weak and was losing hearts.

Phoebe struck the caped villain with her diamond sword, but he grabbed another bottle of potion from his inventory and splashed it on her.

"Stop!" Steve hollered, and he leapt at the caped criminal. With one blow from his diamond sword, he destroyed the caped man.

Two winged soldiers flew high above the gang. Everyone took out their bows and shot arrows at the winged soldiers.

"They keep moving," Maya complained as she shot another arrow. "I keep missing them."

Debbie had great aim. She shot two arrows and destroyed the winged soldiers.

Victoria held the map and said, "The stronghold is right over this mountain. We're almost there."

The gang climbed up the side of the mountain. When they reached the other side, the white snow blinded them.

"Everything is white," said Phoebe.

"I think it's pretty. I wish we could build a snow-man," said Jane playfully.

"This is no time for games," Victoria reminded them. "We have to stop Liam and Dylan."

As Victoria uttered those words, Liam and Dylan emerged from a cave in the side of the mountain and raced toward the group.

"How do you plan on stopping us?" Liam taunted them.

"We control this biome," Dylan said smugly.

"This is where it ends." Liam smiled.

"No." Lucy pointed her diamond sword at Liam. "This is where it ends for you."

Adam splashed a potion of weakness on the two griefers. They called out, "Army! Assemble!"

A horde of men wearing blue jackets burst out of the cave.

"We're outnumbered!" Lucy took a deep breath.

"I have a plan," Jane called out.

Chapter 11
POTIONS AND PORTALS

Jane splashed a potion of invisibility on her friends. "It's my last bit of potion, so let's make it work."

The invisible gang ran toward the griefer group and attacked the men in blue jackets. They had to work fast, since the potion's potency would wear off quickly. Lucy struck three men with her diamond sword and destroyed them, but the number of soldiers wasn't diminishing.

"They're respawning in the cave!" Phoebe cried out.

Maya was battling four soldiers when Debbie swiftly swept in and annihilated the jacketed griefers. Debbie said, "Maya, do you have TNT in your inventory?"

"Yes," Maya said as her sword pierced the arm of a soldier.

"Great. Come with me," ordered Debbie.

"Where are you going?" asked Maya. "You know I can't see you."

"To the cave," whispered Debbie. "We have to blow it up. It's our only chance for survival."

Maya hoped she was following Debbie as she entered the cave. She stopped when she heard a familiar voice nearby. The voice cried out in pain. "Lucy?" Maya asked. "Is that you?"

"Yes," Lucy replied. "I've been weakened from the battle and I don't have any more potions of healing, or any milk, in my inventory. I think this is the end."

"Listen to the sound of my voice. I have potions. I can help you," Maya said to her friend.

Lucy followed the sound of Maya's voice. When she reached her, Lucy began to reappear.

"We're visible," Maya announced. "You need to drink this potion very quickly. We have to work fast."

Lucy gulped the potion. "What are we doing near the cave?""

Maya and Lucy looked at their friends, who were still immersed in battle. Maya replied, "We're going to blow the cave up."

"I have a bunch of TNT in my inventory," Lucy told Maya.

"Great," Maya exclaimed. "So do I."

"Maya!" Debbie's voice boomed through the airy cave. "Where are you? I need your help!"

"Oh no, Debbie's in trouble!" Maya sprinted into the cave, and Lucy followed.

Lucy gasped as she entered the dark cave. It was filled with endless rows of beds. "How many soldiers do Liam and Dylan have working with them?"

"Help!" Debbie cried.

Lucy couldn't see Debbie, and neither could Maya. Lucy called out, "Maya, where are you?"

"Liam has me!"

Liam laughed. "And I'm going to destroy her!"

Lucy and Maya ran deeper into the cave, but there were still no signs of Debbie.

"Where could she be?" asked Maya.

"I see her!" Lucy sprinted toward a door in the cave. She had spotted Debbie's foot.

The duo rushed toward the door. Lucy called, "Liam, you better let our friend go."

"Never!"

Lucy slammed her diamond sword into Liam's unarmored chest, destroying him.

"Thanks!" Debbie let out a loud sigh. "That was scary."

"How come he wasn't wearing any armor?" Maya mused.

"He's very confident, which is his downfall," Debbie said.

"Or he wanted to be destroyed, so he could respawn somewhere else," said Lucy.

They all paused.

Maya said, "We have to destroy these evil griefers. We will show them they are weak."

Debbie grabbed bricks of TNT and placed them throughout the cave. As Lucy placed a brick of TNT near a row of beds, she thought she saw Liam respawning in a bed by the door.

"We have to ignite the TNT now!" Lucy shouted to her friends.

The three girls placed as many bricks of TNT as they could around the cave, and ignited them. They barely made it out of the cave without being destroyed by the explosion.

Kaboom!

Smoke filled the cave. As Lucy and her friends fled the cave, they saw Dylan standing in front of them with a diamond sword. He was wearing armor.

"You destroyed my friend. This is unforgivable."

"We don't want to be forgiven," Lucy called out. "We want you to stop terrorizing the Overworld."

As Lucy spoke, Maya and Debbie grabbed potions of harming and splashed them on Dylan.

"Stop!" he cried out. "I'm weak!"

"And you have no place to respawn," Lucy said as she plowed into Dylan with her diamond sword, destroying the griefer.

The others were still battling Liam and Dylan's griefer army. The trio joined their friends in battle.

Lucy spotted a purple cape in the distance. While destroying a griefer with her diamond sword, she called out, "I see the caped criminal."

The others caught a glimpse of the man.

"We have to follow him," said Lucy.

"How?" Adam asked breathlessly. Everyone was battling the remaining griefer army. How could they abandon the battle they were in to fight another, more powerful, criminal?

Lucy splashed potions of weakness on the griefers, struck them with her diamond sword, and battled the army until the end.

"We're letting him get away!" Lucy was upset. Two griefers struck Lucy with their diamond swords, and she grew weaker. The man in the cape had distracted her, and it was taking a toll on her fighting skills.

"Just concentrate on our battle," Phoebe told her friend, aiming her bow and arrow at the caped man.

"We're too far away," said Lucy. "Don't waste your arrow."

Phoebe knew her friend was right. She kept fighting the soldiers and tried to forget about the caped man.

When the last soldier was destroyed, Lucy led her friends to the spot where she had last seen the villain.

As they trudged through the snow, Jane suggested, "We have to make some snowballs before we leave this biome."

Lucy called out, "I see the caped criminal. He's building a portal to the Nether."

Maya nodded. "Then we definitely need to collect snowballs."

Chapter 12
NOT THE NETHER

While Phoebe gathered snowballs, Lucy crafted a portal to the Nether. Purple smoke rose from the portal.

"Hop on!" Lucy called to her friends.

Phoebe fumbled as she placed a snowball in her inventory. "Wait for me," she called out, but it was too late. She was left behind.

When the group emerged in the Nether, Lucy looked around. "Where's Phoebe?"

Jane replied, "I'm afraid she's still in the cold biome."

"But we can't just leave her!" Lucy was upset.

"Should we go back?" asked Jane.

"Yes," Lucy said, and she looked at the others, hoping they would agree.

"Um," Maya stammered. "I don't think we should."

"I agree," Victoria said. "There's no time."

Stefan protested, "But we can't leave her behind."

"This is a battle, and we all have to watch out for ourselves," Victoria responded.

"How can you say that?" Lucy was shocked.

Jane picked up obsidian from her inventory. "I'm crafting a portal."

"Ouch!" Steve cried out.

"Oh, no!" Lucy looked up and saw three winged griefers gliding above them. They shot arrows at the gang.

Adam took out his bow and arrow and aimed at the flying griefers.

The caped griefer sprinted toward them, his shield-carrying soldiers close behind. "You can't escape now."

Jane stopped crafting the portal and grabbed her diamond sword from her inventory, spinning to pummel into a soldier.

A fireball flew through the sky and landed near Lucy. She narrowly escaped the dangerous, explosive ball.

"Ghasts!" Lucy shouted.

Lucy's heart began to race. She remembered her teacher, Eitan, instructing her to use her fists to fight ghasts. She made a fist and struck the fireball that flew in her direction. It struck the ghast and destroyed it.

"Good job," someone called out. She could swear it was Eitan's voice that spoke to her. Lucy quickly turned around and saw her old teacher standing next to Phoebe.

"Phoebe! Eitan!" Lucy exclaimed, but there was no time for happy reunions. Ghasts were shooting fireballs at her as winged griefers shot arrows at her friends.

"Help me!" Lucy called out to her friends.

Phoebe used her fist to destroy one ghast with its fire-ball, and Eitan destroyed the remaining mobs.

"How did you two find each other?" Lucy asked as she aimed her bow and arrow at a winged griefer.

Phoebe replied, "Eitan was also fighting Liam and Dylan in the cold biome. He saw me making a portal to the Nether, and I asked him to join me."

Victoria and Stefan saw Eitan in the distance and called out, but they were too busy battling the flying griefers to come over to him.

Eitan sprinted toward Victoria and Stefan, helping them battle the pesky griefers. With his bow and arrow, Eitan destroyed the winged griefers.

"Wow! You're a warrior," Phoebe exclaimed. "I'm glad I found you in the cold biome."

Eitan smiled. "Thanks. I just want this battle to be over. We have a graduation to plan."

Lucy sighed. "That seems like it's never going to happen."

"It will," Eitan reassured her.

Adam cried out for help. He was battling the caped griefer and was losing hearts. Lucy ran over to her friend and helped him. She crashed into the caped griefer, pushing him into a pool of lava.

There were several soldiers left in the Nether. Since these soldiers carried shields, they were hard to battle. Debbie, one of the most skilled fighters at Minecrafters Academy, was having trouble.

Eitan, Maya, Phoebe, Jane, Victoria, Stefan, Steve, Adam, and Lucy helped battle the remaining soldiers.

When the last soldier was destroyed, they all drank potions to regain their strength.

"Do you think the battle is over?" asked Phoebe.

"I wish," said Lucy. "I have no idea where these griefers are going to strike next."

"We have to build a portal back to the Overworld," said Phoebe.

"Yes, and this time we all have to get on it," joked Maya, looking pointedly at Phoebe.

"I don't think we have time to build a portal," Jane warned them. "Look up!"

A group of blazes flew through the sky. Their black eyes and yellow skin stood out in the Nether landscape.

"There must be a Nether fortress nearby," said Eitan.

"Well, I'm not going to look for it," said Phoebe as she grabbed a snowball from her inventory and aimed it at the blaze.

The gang had inventories full of snowballs; they were prepared for this battle with the fiery beasts.

Lucy picked up the blaze rods and glowstone dust as the blazes were destroyed and dropped them.

"We need to build a portal now," exclaimed Phoebe.

Within seconds the gang had built and was standing on a portal, surrounded by purple mist. Lucy wondered where they would emerge in the Overworld.

Chapter 13
SNEAKY CREEPERS

The portal left them in the center of Steve's village—and in the middle of a creeper attack.

"Lucy! It's been nonstop since you left. Someone is spawning creepers," Kyra explained while she leapt away from an exploding creeper.

"We are trying to track down the spawner," explained Max.

"But we can't seem to find it," added Henry.

Thunder boomed. Rain fell on the village. As a lightning bolt shot through the town, it hit a creeper.

"A charged creeper!" Steve cried in terror.

A charged creeper was more powerful than a normal creeper. As many of the creepers were struck by lightning bolts, the gang was frightened.

Zombies and skeletons spawned in the rainy weather. "Stand back," Lucy warned them.

Kaboom! A skeleton's arrow struck a charged creeper. The rain flooded the town, as more zombies and skeletons spawned. Lightning struck again, charging more creepers.

"We're in trouble!" Phoebe was shaking, and her voice had a desperate quality. "How are we going to get out of this?"

"We will," Lucy promised her, and she grabbed her diamond sword and rushed through the rain to strike two skeletons.

Jane and Maya fought alongside Lucy. They used all of their strength to battle the bony mobs.

Kaboom!

"Kyra!" Steve shouted.

A silent creeper had destroyed Kyra, and everyone was upset.

Max called out, "Don't worry. We built a large house where Kyra will respawn."

Lucy tried to brush the rain from her eyes. She needed to see so she could battle the four zombies that lumbered toward her.

Adam splashed a potion on the zombies as Lucy pummeled them with her diamond sword.

"We make a good team," Lucy said when they destroyed the vacant-eyed zombies.

"More creepers!" Adam said as the quiet green mob entered the village. "We have to find the spawner."

Lucy and Adam ran down the village streets in search of the spawner. "Do you think it's in one of the village shops?" asked Lucy.

"I have no idea where the spawner is, but I know we have to deactivate it. It's our only hope of surviving this battle," Adam replied as he searched the buildings for the spawner.

"I think I see it," Lucy called from the library.

"Lucy!" a frightened voice cried.

"Avery?" asked Lucy.

"Yes," she replied. "I'm behind a bookshelf."

"Are you okay?" asked Lucy

Adam rushed into the library. "It's here! The spawner is in here."

Lucy stood next to Avery. "We're going to stop this battle and restore peace to the Overworld."

Avery smiled. "Thank you."

"But you have to leave the library as we deactivate this spawner. It could be very dangerous," Lucy informed Avery.

As Avery exited the library, Lucy warned her to watch out for zombies. Lucy walked over to Adam.

"Do you have a torch?" Adam asked as he worked on deactivating the spawner without getting blown up by creepers.

"Yes." Lucy took out a torch and handed it to Adam.

"Almost done," he said as he deactivated the spawner.

Outside thunder boomed throughout the village. They could hear the rain pounding on the library's roof. Lucy cried, "I bet there is lightning outside, and it's charging the rest of the creepers."

"Okay," Adam smiled. "I deactivated the spawner."

The creeper invasion was over, but the battle was far from done. The soggy streets were filled with charged creepers, zombies, and skeletons. As Lucy ran out of the library to inform her friends that the spawner had been deactivated, an arrow pierced her back. Lucy turned to see two skeletons, and for a moment she was relieved that the arrow was from a bony beast and not from a griefer's bow. The village was filled with hostile mobs, and Lucy wasn't sure she'd be able to battle griefers at the same time.

"Lucy!" Phoebe shouted.

Lucy sprinted to Phoebe, who was in the middle of battling three zombies and two skeletons. Lucy struck the zombies, but they weren't losing hearts.

"These are tough zombies," Lucy said as she hit them again and still hadn't destroyed them.

Jane and Maya rushed to their side and battled the zombies and skeletons. As Lucy struck a zombie, the rain stopped and the sun came out.

"Is everyone okay?" Lucy called through the village streets.

Adam announced, "We deactivated the creeper spawner."

Everyone cheered, but stopped as Victoria and Stefan rushed into the center of the crowd.

Stefan said, "I saw the caped creeper. He's on the shore."

Victoria announced, "And he's with Liam and Dylan."

Chapter 14
WATERWAYS

The gang, along with the entire population of the town, sprinted toward the shore to capture the three griefers, but when they arrived, they saw each griefer sail away on their own wooden boat.

"We have to get them!" Lucy shouted.

Kyra called out, "I have boats. I made a bunch recently."

"Enough for everyone?" questioned one of the townspeople.

"No, I don't think we should all chase after the griefers. I think most of us should stay here and protect the village from any hostile mobs and these griefer's soldiers."

The group agreed. Kyra led a handful of people to the building where she stored her boats.

Lucy counted the boats. "You only have five."

Victoria eyed the coast. "We have to get aboard a boat soon, or we're going to lose them."

Kyra ordered, "Lucy, Phoebe, Maya, Jane, and Debbie. These boats are for you. Get on board and save us from the griefers."

The girls hopped on the boats and sailed off on the ocean. Lucy called to the others, "We need to sail as fast as we can."

Everyone picked up speed. They were trailing the griefers. Lucy could see the caped man jump overboard.

"Is he jumping overboard?" she asked.

"Yes," responded Jane, "and it looks like Liam and Dylan jumped into the water, too."

"Their boat is empty," confirmed Lucy.

"Does everyone have a potion of water breathing?" Lucy asked her friends in the neighboring boats.

"Yes," they replied in unison.

"We have to drink now."

The group drank their potions.

"See you under the sea," Lucy said, and she plunged into the deep blue water. At first the swim was refreshing, but once she spotted an elder guardian swimming past her, Lucy's heart began to race. She knew the griefers must have jumped under the water to loot an underwater temple, and she didn't want to battle guardians, elder guardians, and griefers. But she had no choice.

"I see the griefers," Jane said as she swam. "They are outside an ocean monument."

"Watch out, Lucy!" Phoebe called to her friend.

Lucy tried to swim as fast as she could, but she was still struck by the rays from the elder guardian, which left her with the Wither effect. Lucy grew very weak and couldn't swim. Trapped and powerless from the Wither effect, she felt as if she was about to be destroyed and respawn. The fish focused on Lucy again and aimed its powerful rays at her.

Maya pushed Lucy out of the way just in time and handed her milk. "Drink this."

Lucy sipped the milk and replenished her energy. "Thanks! We have to get away from the elder guardian."

Debbie aimed her arrow at the elder guardian and struck the powerful fish. She hit the fish three more times, destroying it.

"We need to get to the griefers," Phoebe said and swam toward the ocean monument.

The five girls swam toward the ocean monument, the griefers had already destroyed the guardians that protected the monument. The girls swam inside.

"I bet they're in the room with the gold bricks," said Phoebe.

"I'm sure of it," said Lucy.

They swam deeper into the ocean monument, and Lucy cried out, "No!" A guardian had spotted Lucy and shot a ray at her.

Phoebe shot an arrow at the guardian, and Jane swam toward the fish with her diamond sword. "Got it!"

The guardian was destroyed. Lucy's energy was still low, and she drank the remainder of the milk she had in her inventory.

"How many times am I going to get struck with the Wither effect?" asked Lucy.

"I wish I could answer that question, and I wish I could say that you'd never be struck by a guardian's rays again," Phoebe said as she swam and searched for the griefers.

"I hear something," Lucy whispered.

"Me too! It sounds like Liam," said Phoebe.

The gang of five swam toward the voices. They had their diamond swords in their hands, ready to attack.

Lucy stormed into a room full of gold bricks and struck Liam. Instead of helping Liam, the caped griefer and Dylan swam away.

"Get them!" Lucy screamed as she struck Liam again.

The others followed the griefers. Liam grabbed his sword and struck Lucy.

"Liam, you're weak. You should give up the battle," Lucy said as she shielded herself from his sword.

"No!" Liam laughed. "I'm going to win."

"Your friends abandoned you," Lucy shouted as she struck him repeatedly with her diamond sword.

"I know where they are going. They didn't abandon me."

"Where are they going?" asked Lucy.

"Like I'd tell you." He smiled.

"I'm going to destroy you!"

"Then I'll respawn with my friends," he said. "I don't care."

Lucy used all of her might to strike Liam, and he was destroyed. She realized she was alone in the ocean monument. She swam over to a small stack of gold bricks and placed them in her inventory. As she picked up the last gold bar, an elder guardian swam near her. It shot a ray at Lucy.

"Oh no!" she called out, but there was nobody there to hear her cries or to give her milk. She was all alone and losing hearts. Lucy scanned her inventory, but she didn't have any milk left.

"Help!" she cried out again, but there was no response.

Lucy waited for the Wither effect to lose its power, as she used what little strength she had to battle the elder guardian. But Lucy knew she was going to lose the fight.

"Lucy!" Phoebe called out.

Jane, Debbie, and Maya appeared and skillfully destroyed the elder guardian with their diamond swords.

"We know where the griefers are hiding," Phoebe said as she handed Lucy a potion of healing.

"Drink that quickly. We have to get to Mushroom Island," said Jane.

Chapter 15
ISLAND INVASION

Lucy and her friends swam to the surface. They could see the boats floating on the water, but they were far away from them.

"What are we going to do?" Phoebe cried.

Lucy replied, "We have to swim to the boats."

The water was rough and the friends were exhausted by the time they reached the boats. Lucy barely had enough strength to hop aboard her small wooden vessel. When she was seated in the boat, she grabbed an apple from her inventory and sailed alongside her friends.

"I can see Mushroom Island," Phoebe called out. She was very excited.

"We can't dock our boats on the Island. We have to surprise the griefers," Lucy said as she took a bite from her apple.

The group of five navigated the waters outside the island, and Jane suggested that they ditch the boats and swim to shore.

"That sounds like a good plan," Lucy agreed.

The gang jumped into the cool blue water and swam to the shore. Normally Lucy loved Mushroom Island. It was a peaceful place, with mooshrooms roaming around the landscape, which was dotted with oversized mushrooms sprouting from the ground. But Lucy wasn't excited for this trip to Mushroom Island, because she knew they had to confront all three powerful griefers. If they didn't stop these griefers, the Overworld might be destroyed.

"I don't see them," Jane said as they walked around the small island.

A mooshroom walked past them, and Maya suggested they milk it. "We should take a break and have some mushroom stew. It's so tasty."

Lucy didn't think this was the time for a meal, but she also knew they needed energy. "Okay, if we can do it quickly, we should milk the mooshroom."

Maya and Debbie leaned over and placed a bowl underneath the mooshroom, milking it while the others kept watch.

"I hear something," Jane whispered to her friends.

"Me too," said Lucy.

"It's coming from over there," Phoebe called out. "By the water."

The group spotted the three griefers docking their boats on the shoreline. Liam spoke. "I'm very annoyed that I wasn't able to get all of the gold blocks from the ocean monument."

"Next time, we'll loot the entire monument," replied Dylan.

"Don't worry about small treasures," the caped man explained. "We have bigger plans. Soon we will be the leaders of the Overworld. Then we will have all the treasure we've ever wanted."

"You're right. Who cares about a few gold bars when we will be able to have everything?" Liam grinned.

The five girls didn't know if they should attack or hide behind the mooshroom. They didn't have very long to contemplate a plan of action, because the three griefers saw them.

"We see you!" Liam laughed, and the three evil griefers sprinted toward them with their diamond swords held high.

Lucy took a deep breath. "We can do this," she said to her friends.

"We have no choice." Phoebe looked over at Lucy. "Let's give it our best shot."

Lucy held her diamond sword in one hand and clutched a potion of harming in the other. As Liam advanced toward her, she splashed the potion on him and then struck him with her diamond sword. He grabbed his sword and pierced Lucy's arm, making her cry out in pain.

The girls outnumbered the griefers, and this gave them an advantage. They used their swords and potions to weaken the three griefers, but the battle wasn't easy.

Liam had very few hearts left. Lucy didn't want to destroy him because she wasn't sure where he would respawn.

"Don't destroy any of them," Lucy called to her friends. She didn't have to say anything else; her friends understood what she meant.

Lucy wasn't sure how they were going to trap these griefers, unless she was able to construct a makeshift prison out of bedrock. She looked over at her friends, who were battling Dylan and the caped man. If she left them in charge of Liam, she'd be able to build the prison.

"Fight Liam," Lucy ordered Maya, "but don't destroy him."

As Lucy raced off to build the bedrock prison, she saw Liam sneak a sip from a potion of healing. With renewed energy and great force, he plunged his sword into Maya's arm.

"Lucy! Help!" Maya shrieked.

Lucy had crafted the side of the prison. She didn't know what to do. Should she finish the bedrock jail or help her friend? Lucy quickly constructed another wall, as Maya let out another shrill call for help. Lucy stopped and dashed to her friend's side to strike Liam with her diamond sword.

"Liam," Lucy demanded. "You're coming with me."

"No!" Liam shouted.

Lucy handed Maya a potion of healing. "And you're coming with me, too. You have to watch this evil griefer."

Maya held her sword against Liam as they walked to the bedrock jail. Lucy finished the prison in record time.

She walked Liam into the room. "This is where you're going to stay for now."

Lucy and Maya could hear Liam shouting from the bedrock prison, but they didn't pay attention to his cries. They ran to their friends' sides and helped them lead Dylan and the caped criminal toward the small bedrock house. Once they placed them inside and closed it, Lucy said, "We have to find away to bring them back to Minecrafters Academy, so we can keep an eye on them."

"I think we have a bigger problem!" Phoebe screamed, as numerous boats docked on the shore. Winged griefers, men in blue jackets, and griefers carrying shields walked onto the island.

"We have to fight their army." Maya's voice shook.

Lucy rushed to the shore and screamed, "The battle is over. We have captured your leaders."

The griefers were angry and shouted, "We will free them. You'll never win."

Lucy questioned the griefers, "Why are you fighting this battle? Your leaders don't care about you."

This comment infuriated the griefers and they shot a sea of arrows at Lucy. She felt weak, and she was about to be destroyed when she heard the griefers let out a collective shriek. Lucy barely had enough strength to turn around. She wanted to know what horrific sight was behind her.

Lucy turned her head and saw her friends Max, Henry, Steve, Adam, and Kyra standing in front of an army of townspeople. The griefers were outnumbered. The battle was over.

Chapter 16
BACK ON CAMPUS

Arrows flew through the air as the townspeople battled the two griefer armies. The griefers lost their energy and one by one they were destroyed.

"We don't know where they'll respawn." Lucy was concerned.

"Without their leader, they are no threat to us. They don't know how to think for themselves," said Phoebe.

When the last griefer soldier was destroyed, Kyra asked, "Where are the griefer leaders?"

Lucy walked them over to the bedrock prison. "Here they are."

Max asked, "What are we going to do with these villains?"

Lucy suggested, "I think it's best if we keep them in a jail on the Minecrafters Academy campus."

The others agreed.

"But how are we going to get them there?" questioned Henry.

Kyra offered, "I can build boats and we can travel to Minecrafters Academy as a group. Victoria and Stefan are already there, working on rebuilding the campus."

Lucy added, "Or we can force them to TP to the Academy."

"That sounds like a good plan," said Max.

"They have very little energy left. I'll TP them now," Lucy said as she entered the small bedrock prison.

Lucy walked into the bedrock prison and pointed her sword at Liam. "I'm TPing you to Minecrafters Academy."

Dylan interrupted, "No!"

Liam said, "We've been in the prison. It's awful."

"Well, you have no other choice," said Lucy.

The man in the cape stood silently.

Lucy asked, "What's your name?'

"It's not important," he replied.

"I need it."

"I know why you need it, and I'm not going to say."

Dylan looked at the caped man. "It's over. Just tell her."

"You'll be trapped in here alone if you don't tell her. Wouldn't you rather be with us?" asked Liam.

"My name is Owen."

Lucy nodded. "We are going to TP right now." Lucy TPed with the three griefers. As they reappeared at the academy, they saw Victoria and Stefan standing in the center of the campus.

"Lucy!" Stefan grinned and then walked her toward the new prison. "We built this large bedrock prison, and there is no way anybody can escape from this jail. It's extremely secure."

Liam, Dylan, and Owen walked into the bedrock prison. Isaac stood by the door.

"We're roommates again, Isaac," said Liam.

Stefan said, "No, you're not. Isaac is no longer in jail. He is charge of the jail. He's going to make sure you don't leave."

"Isaac? Is that true?" Dylan asked.

"Yes," Isaac replied. "I can't believe what you did to the Overworld. All three of you will be in this jail for a very long time."

Isaac locked the door behind him.

Stefan turned to Lucy. "We have a graduation to plan," he said.

"Seriously?" Lucy asked as she looked around the campus. "How can we have a graduation? The school needs to be rebuilt."

"Eitan has been rebuilding the Great Hall, and it's almost done. That was where we planned on having the graduation ceremony."

Lucy hurried across the campus and stood in front of the Great Hall. The building was almost completed. She called out, "Eitan!"

"Lucy, come inside," Eitan said.

Lucy walked inside, pausing as she looked at the theater where the graduation would take place. "This is amazing. You did all of this by yourself?"

"I had help from some students on campus." Eitan gave Lucy a tour of the Great Hall. "I even rebuilt the rooms where visitors will stay. I have a room for your friends Kyra, Steve, Henry, and Max."

"Wow!" Lucy was thrilled, but then she remembered she had to give a speech. Her heart began to race, and she started to sweat. Now that the battle was over, she was going to have to face an internal battle. She was going to learn how to speak in front of a large crowd and face her stage fright.

Lucy started to mumble. Eitan asked, "What are you saying, Lucy?"

"Nothing." She was embarrassed. She had been practicing her speech.

"Are you nervous about giving the speech?"

"Yes," she confessed.

"After watching you battle ghasts, blazes, and winged griefers in the Nether, I think giving a graduation speech will be a piece of cake for you."

Lucy smiled. She hoped Eitan was right.

Chapter 17
POMP AND CIRCUMSTANCE

"I can't believe it's graduation day!" Phoebe was excited. "I know! Our time at Minecrafters Academy went by so fast," said Jane.

Lucy remarked, "It's our last day together."

"Don't say that. We'll see each other a lot." Jane was heartbroken about leaving her friends.

"Should we have a final lunch together in the dining hall?" asked Lucy.

"Stop saying things like that and using words like 'final.' We are going to see each other once school is over." Jane's eyes swelled with tears.

"I know, but we won't be living together like we are at Minecrafters Academy." Lucy walked toward the dining hall.

As the entered the dining area, Lucy hoped that this would be a peaceful last day. She didn't want to deal with any blackouts or attacks from hostile mobs. She grabbed a piece of cake.

"I'm going to miss this cake. They have the best cake here," Lucy said.

"I know. I am going to miss these buffets. I've gotten lazy here. In the Overworld, I was always hunting for my next meal," remarked Phoebe.

Adam walked over to the trio. He looked at Lucy. "Are you prepared for your speech?"

"I guess so." Lucy took a deep breath. "I'm still nervous."

"Steve, Kyra, Henry, and Max will be coming soon," Adam reminded her. "They are very excited to watch us graduate."

"I hope I don't make a fool of myself when I give the speech," she confessed.

"You're going to be great. Remember when you were my assistant at the talent show? You were very nervous, but you did an incredible job."

"Thanks." Lucy smiled.

Stefan and Victoria entered the dining hall. Victoria announced, "Everyone will meet in the Great Hall after lunch. We are very excited to begin our graduation ceremony."

The students cheered. Stefan walked over to Lucy and her friends. "Lucy, are you ready? You have to get to the Great Hall earlier than the others. We have to go over your speech."

Lucy took a final bite of her cake and nodded. "I'm ready." Although she was still nervous, she knew she had to face her fears.

When she entered the Great Hall, her heart began to race. She stood on the stage and recited her speech to an empty room. It wasn't as hard as she imagined. Lucy decided she would just pretend that the room was empty when she was giving the real speech.

As Lucy prepared backstage, she saw all of the guests enter the Great Hall. Kyra, Steve, Henry, and Max were in the front of the room. They were smiling and ready to watch their friend walk on stage. Lucy's stomach squirmed.

Phoebe walked over to Lucy. "Just think about the big party we have planned after the graduation. We're going to play that disc we got when the skeleton destroyed that charged creeper."

Lucy remembered the disc and the party. She was excited for the party, but it still didn't stop her from being nervous about giving the speech.

Stefan called Lucy's name. It was time. She took a deep breath and walked onto the stage.

"It seems like just yesterday we all started our studies at Minecrafters Academy. I remember how nervous I was for my first day of school. Almost as nervous as I am right now, giving this speech." Lucy paused.

Kyra smiled at Lucy as she delivered the speech. Lucy realized that giving the speech wasn't as hard as she imagined. She actually enjoyed it. When everyone applauded, Lucy felt a sense of pride and accomplishment. She had faced her fears.

Chapter 18
GRADUATION PARTY

"It's time for our party!" Phoebe exclaimed.

Everyone raced to the party, which took place in the center of campus, and had tables of food and drinks.

"This is a really great party," Kyra said to Lucy. "I bet it's going to be hard for you to leave the academy."

"Yes, it is." Lucy was upset that she was leaving her friends, but she was glad that order was restored in the Overworld and she could return to Steve's peaceful wheat farm.

Steve, Henry, and Max ran toward Lucy. Henry said, "You gave a great speech."

"Thanks!" Lucy smiled.

Max asked, "Are you ready to go on a treasure hunt? I heard there is a large pile of treasure in a jungle temple not far from here."

"That sounds like fun," Lucy replied. She was happy to start another adventure. Although it was hard to leave her school, she always knew there would be something exciting happening in the future.

Phoebe offered Lucy a piece of cake. "I'm having such a great time at this party. And I have to let you know that you gave the best speech."

Max asked Phoebe, "Do you want to join us on a treasure hunt?'

"A treasure hunt! That sounds like fun," exclaimed Phoebe.

"Yes, come with us!" Lucy was thrilled Phoebe was joining her on the treasure hunt. "We have to ask Jane if she can come, too."

Lucy and Phoebe found Jane talking to a group of fellow graduates. Lucy asked, "Would you like to go on a treasure hunt?"

"Yes," Jane replied, "of course."

Lucy was so happy that her two best friends from the academy would join her old friends on a treasure hunt in the jungle.

Stefan, Victoria, and Eitan came over to Lucy and her friends. They wanted to say goodbye and wish them well in the Overworld.

"I'm going to miss Minecrafters Academy," Lucy told them.

"You can always come and visit," said Victoria.

"There will always be a room for you in the Great Hall," added Eitan.

"You have been a very important person in this school's history," Stefan told Lucy, "and we want you to know how much you mean to us."

Lucy told them about her treasure hunt with Phoebe and Jane. "I made new friends and I learned valuable skills at this school. I will always remember my time here."

Everyone ate cake and danced to the music from the disc. It was the ultimate graduation party. Lucy spotted Adam. "Do you want to join us on a treasure hunt?" she asked him.

"A treasure hunt? Yes. I need to replenish my inventory."

Lucy was even more pleased that all of her friends would be on this new adventure with her. She knew that when the party was over, she would still be surrounded by the people she cared about, and that made her very happy.

When the party ended, Lucy and her friends left Minecrafters Academy. They walked through the large gates that stood at the entrance to the Academy.

Lucy studied the map. "You're right, Steve. The jungle isn't far from here."

"Yes, it's just over the mountain," Steve remarked.

The gang climbed up the side of the mountain. They stopped at the top.

Lucy looked at the Minecrafters Academy campus and smiled. She knew she'd be back one day.

DO YOU LIKE FICTION FOR MINECRAFTERS?

Check out other unofficial Minecrafter adventures from Sky Pony Press!

nvasion of the
Overworld
MARK CHEVERTON

Battle for the
Nether
MARK CHEVERTON

Confronting the
Dragon
MARK CHEVERTON

Trouble in
Zombie-town
MARK CHEVERTON

The Quest for
the Diamond
Sword
WINTER MORGAN

The Mystery
of the Griefer's
Mark
WINTER MORGAN

The Endermen
Invasion
WINTER MORGAN

Treasure
Hunters in
Trouble
WINTER MORGAN

Available wherever books are sold!

DO YOU LIKE FICTION FOR MINECRAFTERS?

Read the rest of the Unofficial Minecrafters Academy series!

Zombie Invasion   Skeleton Battle   Battle in the
WINTER MORGAN   WINTER MORGAN   Overworld
                                      WINTER MORGAN

DO YOU LIKE FICTION FOR MINECRAFTERS?

Read the Unofficial Minetrapped Adventure series!

Trapped in the Overworld
WINTER MORGAN

Mobs in the Mine
WINTER MORGAN

Terror on a Treasure Hunt
WINTER MORGAN

Ghastly Battle
WINTER MORGAN

Creeper Invasion
WINTER MORGAN

Attack of the Ender Dragon
WINTER MORGAN

Available wherever books are sold!